Suspended: The Beginning

Suspended: The Beginning

THE PAST LIFE PRISM SERIES TIME TRAVEL SUSPENSE

BOOK ONE

JULIE BAWDEN DAVIS

Roses
A R E
RED
PUBLISHING

Acknowledgments

As they say, it takes a village. Here's my village. I'm supremely grateful to each of these fabulous people!

ARC Reading Gems
Kery Bailey
Julie Schlueter
Susa Fraccaroli
Trish Darrenkamp
Marilyn Smith
Lisa Starkey
Beth Helm
Teresa Reitnauer
Chelle Young
Asra Syed
Jacquelyn Gray
Penny McCulloch
Karen McTyeire

Pros
Judy Bullard, cover design
Kyle Kane, logo design
Sabrina Wildermuth, design consultation

To déjà vu moments that last lifetimes.

Chapter One

September 4, 1998, Chapman University, Orange, California

Sophia Strand eased the door open to the first physics class of the semester and slipped inside as the professor spoke, his voice carrying in the study hall. She slid into the closest seat, gently setting down her backpack, then looked toward the front of the room. When she did so, her eyes met the teacher's gaze. So much for coming in late unnoticed.

For a nanosecond, she thought he might say something, but then he continued. "As I was saying, while physics may make some of you feel like groaning, I assure you this will be a class you will never forget. Contrary to popular misconceptions, physics," he stopped and his eyes came to meet Sophia's once again, then he looked away, "is all about people, places, things, and yes, even animals, for all you pet lovers out there. It is fundamentally about how the universe behaves. And you," he gestured to the class with his arms open, "are the universe—or at least a small piece of the universe. You'll find in the next sixteen weeks that physics is of definite consequence to your life."

He turned his tall, muscular form toward the chalkboard and began jotting something down. He had blond hair and wore jeans and an emerald-green t-shirt, and Sophia noticed that he was a lefty, which somehow made him even more intriguing.

"You'll need several books for the class, including this biography of Isaac Newton," he said as he wrote, his script running upward at a slant. At the end of each sentence, he tapped the chalk on the board several times before moving on.

So entranced was Sophia watching him write that she realized suddenly she hadn't taken out her notebook. She quickly unzipped her backpack and removed a yellow pad and fished out a pen.

When he finished, the professor turned back toward the class and asked, "Can anyone tell me at least one of Isaac Newton's universal laws?" His eyes swept the room.

The student sitting next to Sophia shot up his arm, and the teacher, whose name she hadn't caught since she'd been late, pointed to him.

"The law of motion," said the student.

The teacher leaned against the desk and crossed his arms over his broad chest and nodded. "Very good. Newton came up with three laws of motion. Anyone able to drill down further on this?"

There was a rustling of papers and students shifted in their seats, but no one spoke.

The teacher uncrossed his arms and stood. "Newton's first law of motion is that an object will not change its motion unless a force acts on it. Anyone care to comment on that?" His eyes came to rest on Sophia.

She cleared her throat and said, "Would we call that cause and effect?"

The teacher smiled, his face becoming even more handsome when he did so. "Yes, we could, Miss?"

Sophia's heart did a flipflop when she realized he was asking her name. She cleared her throat again, "Strand."

"There is always an effect when something or someone acts. Always." He reached for a book on his desk and held it up. "This is Einstein's Theory of Relativity. I'm going to read you some selections."

Sophia had a hard time keeping up with the concepts as she watched the teacher read. She enjoyed hearing his voice, though. There was something rhythmic and comforting in how he spoke. Every few paragraphs, he would raise his head and comment on what he'd just read, then ask questions.

Forty-five minutes later when class ended, Sophia slid her pad, which held very little notes, into her backpack. She stood and looked to the front of the room where the teacher was gathering his things. Without thinking, she headed his way.

When she was a few feet from him, he met her gaze, and she noticed he had blue eyes. "Miss Strand, do you have a question?"

Feeling suddenly short of breath, Sophia responded, "I didn't catch your name, as I was late."

He smiled and reached out his hand. "Dr. Farrow."

As Sophia took his hand, she nearly gasped at the jolt that passed through her. For a dizzying second, she saw an image in her mind's eye of the professor on a mountaintop, a mass of people gathered below. Unsure of what was happening, she stood suspended for a moment, struggling to even her breathing. "It's very nice to meet you," she finally mustered.

Dr. Farrow cocked his head slightly, and a small smile turned up the corners of his mouth. When their hands separated, he asked, "This is your first physics class? What's your major?"

"I'm a psych major with a concentration in social work. And yes, my first physics class. I hope I can get the hang of it."

"I'm sure you will." He gestured to the door with the stack of books he held. "I've got to get to my next class."

Sophia felt her face flush. "Of course, forgive me for keeping you." She turned toward the door.

Dr. Farrow followed close behind her. "No need to apologize. The class is across campus, so a bit of a jog. I'm always happy to answer questions. There will be plenty of time for answers. Have a good day, now."

Sophia stopped to get her bearings as she watched him take long strides down the hallway, then disappear out a doorway onto campus.

. . .

After her next two classes, which went by in a blur as she scribbled down notes on all the demands she'd be facing, Sophia made her way to her dorm room, relieved to find the room empty when she arrived. Though her roommate was nice, she was ultra-talkative. Sophia found she couldn't get a word in edgewise, if at all. The constant prattle got on her nerves after a while. Besides, she wanted to sit for a moment and process the morning. Especially physics class.

She pulled open a little fridge and took out a cold water bottle. Sitting down at her desk wedged up against the window, she pulled back the curtain so she could see the quad with its giant green lawn below. As she did so, a vision of Dr. Farrow on the mountaintop flashed before her once again. And then another vision of him in what looked like a military uniform.

"You've got to get it together, Sophia," she whispered to herself. It was times like this, when the world seemed unsteady under her and as if she might slip sideways at any moment that Sophia wished she could call her mother. The grief counselor had said these were normal reactions to losing someone—that grief could do strange things—but Sophia felt there was something more. She took out the Nokia cellphone her father had given her only for emergencies and made a call to a familiar number.

"Yes, my little love. I am so happy you called."

"Grandmother, you are well?" As she said this, Sophia pictured her grandmother sitting on the balcony of her seaside home in Greece. She heard the gulls squawking.

"I am, but you are not. Tell me, what is happening?"

"The visions. They are back. But this time, not of mother."

"What has happened?"

"I saw some things when I met someone. When I shook his hand. A professor."

"Ahh." She could almost hear her grandmother thinking. "That is why."

Sophia felt the familiar wave of discomfort followed by curiosity sweep through her. "What is why?"

"When you touched, you made the age-old connection. That will bring the visions, the memories of other times and places. As we've

4

talked about before, it is best to allow the visions to come, rather than fight them."

"But I don't understand, where do they come from?" Sophia knew this call would cost a fortune, and she would have to endure her father's anger over it.

A bell clanged on her grandmother's end. "I must go. My client has arrived. You already know the answer to your question, Sophia."

Chapter Two

"Miss Strand, are you listening?"

Sophia looked up from her notebook to see her social work practice teacher staring at her.

"I'm sorry, no, what was the question?"

"In last night's reading assignment, *A Child Called It*, how did that strike you? The use of the word it to describe a human being?"

Sophia swallowed. She had read some of the reading assignment, but the abuse the little boy had suffered at the hands of his mother bothered her so deeply, she had started to cry and stopped reading. "To be perfectly honest, I found it horrible and terribly sad."

The teacher, an older woman with jet-black hair streaked with gray, sighed. "That is a perfectly natural response to one of the most horrific child abuse cases in California history, but..." She held up the book they were speaking about. "That is not the type of response that will hold you in good stead in this line of work. You will see many sad and horrific things as a social worker, as well as cases of neglect, where children are left to fend for themselves. You can't," she said, punctuating the air with the book, "get personally involved. If you do, I promise you, it will be the end of you in the end. I've seen it happen."

"But what about compassion?" Sophia heard herself saying.

The teacher put down the book and answered. "Compassion is a good thing, providing it doesn't turn into empathy. If you are the type of person who feels other's feelings and can't let them go, this may not be the best line of work for you." As she finished her sentence, the teacher's eyes came to rest on Sophia.

Sophia left social work class a half hour later, the teacher's comments about feeling other's feelings reverberating in her head. Didn't everyone feel other's feelings? You would think that would be a good thing. Oh, she was so confused. She'd heard that going away to college was tough, but she thought they were talking about being away from friends and family. She'd always been a good student, and since her junior year in high school thought she'd be a social worker. Now she discovers she may not be suited for the work? Of course, she reminded herself, that was just one person's opinion, and yet, the woman had been a social worker for twenty-five years. If Sophia was being honest with herself, what she said made sense in a way.

She headed to the school cafeteria. It was nearly lunchtime, and she found she could usually reason things out better after having a bite to eat.

As she stood in line waiting for her turn to order a burger, the smell of French fries wafting toward her, she sensed someone behind her. Turning, she came face to face with Dr. Farrow. In the fluorescent light of the cafeteria, she could see that he appeared younger than she'd first thought.

He smiled, his eyes lighting up. "We meet again."

Sophia took a breath to ease the fluttering in her chest at standing this near him. "Dr. Farrow. I guess it's lunch time for you?"

"It is," he said. "And you can call me Phillip. Dr. Farrow sounds so old."

Sophia laughed.

"There you go," he said. "I knew there was a smile under that frown. You're a freshman?"

Sophia blushed. "It's that obvious?"

He grabbed some silverware from the dispensers as they inched their way toward the short order cook. "You have that new, nervous glow about you. But that's not a bad thing," he added quickly. "I wasn't here too long ago in your shoes."

Sophia was struggling to form a response when the cook asked, "What can I get you?"

"I'll take a burger and fries."

"How you want your burger?"

"Well done, please."

The cook raised his eyebrows at Phillip.

"I'll have the same as her," he said, "but make my burger medium." He glanced around the cafeteria. "Did you want to find a seat?"

Was he asking her to eat lunch with him? "Yes, that sounds good," she squeaked.

He walked ahead of her, and as he did so, a vision of him cutting through dense jungle terrain flashed through her mind, then left just as quickly. He sat down at a table and gestured to the chair across from him.

"So, you're majoring in social work. How do you like it?" he asked as she took her utensils and water bottle off her tray.

"Well, I thought I liked it. But today in class..." She stopped, suddenly aware that she was about to share something very personal.

He opened his water bottle and took a long drink, then plunked it down on his tray. "Not such a good day?"

Sophia grasped her water bottle; the cold felt good against her hot palms. "The teacher said something I hadn't considered before."

"What's that?"

"That it's not a good thing to have empathy in that line of work."

His eyes became thoughtful. "I can see how that might throw you off. You don't think you can do it? Not have empathy?"

Sophia was surprised at how he answered her so directly. Usually, that would bother her, but somehow it was okay coming from him.

She rolled the water bottle between her hands before answering. "If I'm going to be honest with myself, no, I don't think I can."

The cook called out their order then, and Phillip shot out of his seat. "I'll get them." He returned moments later and handed her a plate piled with fries and a burger. "Nothing a burger can't cure."

Sophia laughed again, and dug in.

. . .

Back in her room at the end of the day, Sophia sat down at her desk. Ever since her lunch with Phillip, she hadn't been able to get him out of her head. There was something about him. About them sitting there at the lunch table together that felt so familiar. So right. She knew that if she said this out loud, it would sound crazy. A freshman crush on her cute physics teacher. Could she be any more stereotypical?

Sophia pulled out her algebra book and opened it up. Ugh. She really didn't like math. It was so boring and hard to remember, but she had to work twice as hard on it if she was going to keep her scholarship.

After studying calculations for some time, her eyes became so heavy and the fatigue so great that she could no longer think clearly, so she set down her pencil and climbed into bed. The day had turned to twilight, the only light her desk lamp. She closed her eyes. Just for a moment, she'd rest.

Sophia was dreaming. She looked down at her clothing to find she wore an exquisite gown made of sky-blue silk, accented with silver brocade. Violin music strained in the distance, and she was walking down a hallway toward a winding staircase. The floor was carpeted, and her heels dug in as she walked. Stopping in front of a large mirror to check out her reflection, she tucked stray wisps of black hair into the chignon at the back of her neck. Then she turned toward the staircase, grasping her dress in one hand. As she took hold of the alabaster banister and began descending, the music heightened to a crescendo. She glanced down at the foot of the stairs, her heart somersaulting. There he stood, Randall, waiting for her, dressed in a red and white uniform, his broad, black and white cap in his hands. He smiled at her, his blue eyes flashing.

The overhead light switched on in the dorm room, startling Sophia out of her slumber. She sat up in bed, blinking and shielding her eyes.

"Shoot, I'm sorry," said her roommate. "I didn't know you were in here."

"It's okay," said Sophia. "I need to get back to my homework." She was about to slide out of bed when she remembered the dream. The man waiting at the foot of the stairs was Phillip.

Chapter Three

S ophia stood outside of physics class the next day seconds before class started. She hadn't slept well last night, concerned that she would make a fool of herself in front of Phillip in class today. Another student approached then and reached for the doorknob. She took a deep breath, then followed her in.

Once seated, Sophia looked to the front of the room, surprised to see an older woman sitting at the desk. After checking the clock on the wall, the woman stood and addressed the class. "My name is Dr. Reynolds. Dr. Farrow's schedule has changed. He won't be teaching this course after all. I will be."

At the teacher's announcement, Sophia felt a mixture of relief and disappointment.

"What is it, Sophia?" Her mother blinked her eyes open in the dim light, and her father stirred in the bed beside her.

"I had a bad dream. Can I sleep with you?" asked Sophia, seven at the time.

Her mother sat up and whispered, "Let's go to your room. I'll stay with you there."

Sophia padded softly out of the room, and her mother followed, closing the door quietly behind them.

"Do you want some milk? It might help you sleep," she asked.

Sophia shook her head. "I'm not thirsty."

Her mother took her hand as they walked to Sophia's room where three nightlights glowed, their light casting long shadows.

"Lie down," her mother instructed. Sophia did as she was told, then her mother climbed in with her. "Tell me, what was the dream about?"

"I saw papa on a giant horse, and you were crying. He looked funny. He had a sword."

"Go on," her mother said.

"I think you were sad, because he was leaving, like he does now."

Her mother sighed. "We've talked about this. Your father has an important job with the government."

"I know, mama. And there was something else." Sophia angled her small body so she could meet her mother's eyes.

"What was it?"

"I had a baby sister. You let me hold her. She was so tiny."

At the look in her mother's eyes, Sophia felt her chest constrict. "What is it, mama?"

"Let's not talk about your dream anymore, okay. It's only making you more upset. Close your eyes and get some sleep. It will all be gone by morning."

It wasn't until a spring day her last semester of college that Sophia saw Dr. Farrow again. She was walking through the quad with a friend discussing graduation plans, when she looked up to see him heading toward them, several books under one arm. When their eyes met, she felt a jolt that caused her to gasp and stop walking.

"Sophia, you okay?" she heard her friend say, but she was stuck in place.

Dr. Farrow stopped in front of them. "Sophia, how are things going for you?" he asked.

Sophia cleared her throat and replied, "I'm doing well, Dr. Farrow. I'll be graduating in May." She gestured to her friend. "This is Vivian. She's also graduating."

Dr. Farrow nodded at Vivian. "Nice to meet you," he said, then shifted the books from one arm to the other and addressed Sophia. "If I may ask, what major did you decide on? The last time we spoke, you were reconsidering social work, I think it was."

He remembered. "I decided to go into general counseling, instead."

"From your expression, it looks like you made the right choice?"

Sophia smiled. "I think I did."

"Do you have a job lined up for after college?"

"I have a few interviews soon, but nothing set up," she said.

He reached into his pocket and pulled out a card. "Here's my number. I know someone who runs a counseling center. I believe she's hiring."

"Thank you so much," said Sophia.

"Of course, I've got to get to a class. Talk to you soon." And then he was off.

"Oh, my god, he's gorgeous," said Vivian under her breath. "And he knows your name. I think he likes you."

Sophia felt her face flush. "I doubt that. He's just being nice."

Her friend chuckled. "Okay, sure, if you say so."

By the following day, Sophia had gotten up the nerve to call Dr. Farrow. She dialed the phone, her hand shaking slightly as she waited for him to answer.

"Hello?"

"Dr. Farrow. This is Sophia Strand. You told me to call you about the possible job at the counseling center."

"I'm glad you called. She does need someone at her counseling center and would love to take on a new graduate. How about if I meet you there today? Do you have time?"

"I, yes, I can make time," said Sophia, practically stuttering in surprise as she took down the counseling center information, located within walking distance of the university.

Thirty minutes later, she was walking up the steps to a craftsman style building on Chapman Avenue in Old Towne Orange. She'd changed into her interview outfit, a black knee-length skirt and pumps with a lavender blouse. She had pulled her shoulder-length black hair back with a barrette and wore the black pearl earrings her grandmother had given her for her eighteenth birthday. When she pushed open the door, which had a plaque on it that read Kline Counseling Center, the door chimed. She walked into a hushed, empty waiting room and glanced at her wristwatch. She was five minutes early. As she sat down to wait, she noticed for the first time the murmur of voices coming from another room. At the top of the hour, she heard movement in the hallway and before long the waiting room door swung open. A man walked through and left out the front door, and a woman entered the waiting room. "You must be Sophia."

Sophia stood quickly and jutted out her hand. "I am. And I apologize, but Dr. Farrow didn't tell me your name. Is it Dr. Kline?"

The woman's face lit up with a broad smile. She wore her brown hair short and had on a navy blue suit and white blouse. Around her neck hung a gold chain with a small locket. "Kline was my mentor's name. I took over his practice several years ago. I'm Dr. Cathy Harlan. It's so nice to meet you. Phillip says great things about you. I understand you are about to graduate from Chapman? They have an excellent counseling program."

"That's right," said Sophia, glancing at the front door.

"If I know Phillip, he'll come barreling through the door any minute. Let's go into my office and have a chat."

"Have you known Dr. Farrow for long?" asked Sophia as she followed her down a short hallway and into a sunny office.

"Yes, most definitely. Phillip is my brother. Harlan is my married name."

Sophia's face must have registered shock, because Dr. Harlan laughed. "I guess that's not information he shared with you?" She gestured to a chair across from a desk.

Sophia sat and cleared her throat. "To be honest, Dr. Farrow and I barely know each other. We met my freshman year briefly, and then I ran into him the other day on campus."

Dr. Harlan laughed again. "That's my brother for you!"

Embarrassment washed through Sophia, who motioned to stand. "I'm sorry for the confusion, Dr. Harlan. I—"

The woman raised a palm, her expression becoming serious. "First of all, call me Cathy. And secondly, my brother is a good judge of character, so if he says I should talk to you, there is a good reason."

Sophia sat back in the chair.

"Let's start with your major and what you've studied these last four years, then tell me about the practicum hours you've completed."

It was at the end of the interview when Cathy and Sophia were working out the details of her coming to work at the center following graduation that Phillip came barging into the office. "I'm so sorry. I got hung up." He looked from one woman to the other. "It looks like it went well?"

Cathy chuckled. "It did. We're all done. Meet the newest member of the Kline counseling team."

"That's great!" Phillip beamed. "How about we go out for dinner to celebrate."

"I've got plans with Chuck," said Cathy.

Phillip looked to Sophia. "What about you? Are you free?"

His invitation set her heart to pitter pattering so hard, she could barely think. What day was it? Did she have any classes tonight? Finally, she managed to say, "I'm free."

"Let's go then," he said. "My treat."

As they left the office, Sophia suddenly understood the expression, walking on a cloud.

Chapter Four

"The physics class you were going to teach my freshman year. What happened?"

They were at a Mediterranean restaurant near the office Phillip had suggested. Sophia took a sip of iced tea, watching as his brow furrowed, then he grinned. "It's top secret. If I told you, I'd have to...well, you know."

Sophia didn't know what to make of the comment. Was he joking? Or was it really something he couldn't talk about? She took another sip of tea, then reached for the pita in the basket between them and tore off a piece, dipping it into garlic humus.

"Do you always give up this easily?" he asked.

She took a napkin and wiped some humus off the side of her cheek. "What do you mean?"

"No more questions about where I was?"

"I figure you are either joking or there's a reason why you're not telling me, so what else is there to ask?"

"Well, if you put it that way, then maybe I will tell you."

"Okay," said Sophia, moving her water glass out of the way so the waitress could set down her falafel.

"All kidding aside, I'm in the National Guard. Since the class was on

Fridays, and I have monthly training exercises over the weekend, it wasn't going to work with my schedule."

"Oh, that's interesting. From what I understand, you could be called in if we had a war, right? Like the reserves?"

"Exactly." He gestured to her plate. "Go ahead and eat. I'm sure mine will be here soon. So, tell me about Sophia Strand. Are you from Southern California?"

Sophia picked up a pita and put the falafel inside, dashing yogurt dressing on top before wrapping it up. "Menlo Park."

"The Bay area. Very nice."

The waitress set down his plate of stuffed grape leaves, and he dug in. They ate in silence, Sophia stealing glances at him as he ate. He was so handsome. Did he have a girlfriend, she wondered?

When Sophia finished and pushed her plate away, she said, "Thank you again for the introduction to your sister. I'm really excited I'll be working with her."

"I'm glad you enjoyed your meal," he said, nodding appreciatively at her empty plate as he finished his up. "And I'm happy to help. I could tell when you were a freshman that you had potential."

That surprised Sophia. "You did?"

"It's something in the eyes. I don't see it in many students."

Sophia waited, fascinated by this line of thought.

"It's a sense of being present." He picked up his water glass. "To your new job."

They clinked glasses, and as they did so, she saw a flash of Phillip in a business suit holding a champagne glass, his hair darker in color and brushed back. Just as quickly, the image vanished.

She must have had a funny look on her face because he asked, "Something the matter?"

"No, nothing," she said, averting her eyes and removing an imaginary crumb off her blouse.

A half hour later, Phillip dropped Sophia off at her apartment, and she floated inside and shut the door. For a few long minutes, she stood in the entryway, processing the fact that she'd just been to dinner with the most gorgeous man she was sure she'd ever met.

. . .

It wasn't until several weeks after graduation when Sophia was working full-time at Kline Counseling that she saw Phillip again. She'd been dying to know more about him—and on many occasions almost asked Cathy about her brother—but decided it wasn't appropriate while she was trying to make a good impression.

It was a sweltering Southern California late June day and Sophia was overseeing the reception room and incoming clients. When the door chimed, she expected to see the next patient, but instead there stood Phillip in a tank top and jeans, his arms rippled with muscles.

"Sophia," he exclaimed as he came bursting in.

"Your sister is in session."

"It just so happens that I was looking for you."

Sophia felt a rush of delight at his words. "Oh," is all she managed to say as she waited for him to continue.

"When we went out to dinner, you said you enjoy plays."

"I did? I mean, yes, I did."

"There's a play at the university Friday night. Would you like to go? It's a bit on the esoteric side, but I figure you'll understand it. Please tell me you will, so I don't have to go alone."

Sophia took a moment to gather her thoughts after his abrupt invitation. Finally, she answered. "Yes, I would love to go to a play."

"Mama, how did you know that papa was the one?" Sophia was lying in her mother's bed with her after school at the beginning of her senior year of high school.

She started to answer, but then began coughing. Sophia handed her a glass of water and waited while she took several small sips. Then she took it from her mother's unsteady grasp and set it on the bedside table, snuggling back down beside her.

"I knew the moment we met, and I looked into your father's eyes. I can't tell you how I knew. I just knew."

"I hope that happens with me, Mama. That I just know."

Her mother turned her head and smiled, putting her soft hand on Sophia's cheek. "You will. You'll see."

As Sophia got ready for her date that night, she went through a dozen outfits before she decided on a pair of jeans and a silk blouse. She pulled her hair over one shoulder, tying it with a red ribbon to match the shirt. Then she slid her feet into wedge heels and put on her mother's gold hoop earrings. When she finished, she smiled into the mirror. Should she pinch her cheeks? Was this real?

Sophia heard Phillip pull up in his MG, and before long, there was a quick rap on her front door. She took a few breaths before pulling it open.

There Phillip stood, looking as if he'd just jumped out of the shower —his blond hair unruly and damp, white t-shirt and jeans on. She must have been staring, because he put his hands to his head and smoothed back his hair. "I was at the pool. You look pretty. Are you ready to go?"

Had Sophia heard right? He thought she was pretty? She closed the door and took his extended arm, then tried to unscramble her brain as they headed to his car. Say something, Sophia, she urged herself. When he opened the passenger side of the car, she slid in and set her purse on her lap, then began rooting around unsuccessfully for the seatbelt.

"May I? It can be tricky," said Phillip. He pulled the seatbelt out and handed it to her, then shut the door and got into the driver's seat. "All set?" he asked as he turned on the car and headed out of the parking lot.

Once they were on Chapman Avenue headed for the college, Sophia asked, "What is the name of the play?"

Phillip glanced at her and grinned, then drew his attention back to the road and stopped at a light. "I did warn you that it's a bit esoteric. It's called Orca Speaks. The whole play is apparently from the viewpoint of a killer whale."

The nervous tension in Sophia finally spilled over, and she laughed. "You're kidding, right?"

He looked over at her and raised his eyebrows. "No, this is the real thing. One of my students produced the play and is starring in it. I told her I'd go. It sounds odd, but I promised."

Chapter Five

P hillip placed his warm hand on the small of Sophia's back, sending a delicious shiver up her spine as they headed to their seats. Even though the play sounded unusual, she didn't care if it meant being this close to him.

As it turned out, Sophia found the play interesting. The perception of the whale and the whale's search for food was juxtaposed against the backdrop of man's fear of killer whales, and killer animals in general. When those involved in the play had finished and taken their last bows, Phillip announced, "Let's go backstage, and I'll introduce you to Angelica."

Sophia knew she was being silly, but she couldn't help feeling a twinge of jealousy as they headed backstage. Did the fact that Phillip came to see Angelica's play mean she meant something to him?

After they made their way through a throng of students and parents, they stopped just outside of a small circle of people surrounding a tall, reedy girl with short, jet-black hair streaked with silver highlights. She was talking animatedly, so Sophia and Phillip stood back and waited.

"I take it that's Angelica?"

Phillip nodded. "I think you'll like her. She's a senior, so not much younger than you."

Angelica looked their way then as her visitors began to disperse. "Dr. Farrow!"

"That was great," said Phillip.

"Thank you. I'm so glad you could make it." Angelica's face was tinged light gray with stage makeup.

Phillip turned to Sophia. "This is Sophia Strand. She graduated in May. Sophia, Angelica Robertson."

Angelica grinned and thrusted out a hand. "So nice to meet you, Sophia. Thanks for coming. I hope it wasn't too weird." As they shook, Angelica tipped her head to the side and asked, "Have we met before?"

"It's possible," said Sophia, also unsure why Angelica seemed so familiar. They didn't run in the same circles.

"You said you also worked on the sets?" said Phillip.

"I did. That giant ocean wave took forever to paint."

Just then several people approached to congratulate Angelica, and Phillip and Sophia waved goodbye.

Outside under the stars as they walked through campus, Sophia said, "That was very interesting, and it was nice to meet Angelica. Do you always go to student events?"

Phillip stopped and gazed up at the sky, then pointed to a bench. "Want to sit and do some stargazing? It looks like Uranus is out."

As they made themselves comfortable, he answered her question. "Every once in a while when I'm asked to go to an event like a play or exhibit, I do. But I try not to make a habit out of it. Angelica is a kick, though. I figured her play would be worth watching."

It made Sophia feel good knowing she wasn't among a long line of students Phillip was being nice to. She relaxed and leaned back on the bench, checking out the sky. "Show me Uranus."

Phillip pointed to a swath of brilliant stars. "It's the bright planet in the center of that mass of stars. Do you see it?"

Sophia sat up and followed his finger to the sky, seeking out the brightest light. "I think I do," she said, excited. "I usually have no idea what I'm looking at." As she admired the chaos of stars that she now saw held a certain order, she felt Phillip watching her. She turned to him, the intense look in his eyes sending sparks throughout her body.

"You're very pretty," he said. "But I'm sure you hear that often."

Sophia wasn't sure that her voice would work when she replied. "Actually, I don't hear it that often, but thank you."

"I can't imagine why," said Phillip, moving closer to her. *Was he going to kiss her?*

Sophia said nothing, instead sat there suspended, waiting for his next move. She nearly closed her eyes, but instead kept them on his.

"Do you feel like we've known each other before?" he asked her in a low voice.

Still unable to speak, Sophia felt as if her breath had become caught in her throat. She was mustering up the words to answer when he reached out and gently took her face in his hands, pulling her to him. When their lips met, she felt a warm river wash through her. The kiss was tender at first, then became passionate. Sophia responded by wrapping her hands around his neck. Though she'd never been kissed by Phillip, somehow it felt like they had done this before.

When they finished, he was short of breath as he put his forehead to hers. "I need to stop before I do something..." his voice trailed off. "I've wanted to do that since the moment I met you."

"You have?" said Sophia in a much louder tone than she meant to.

Phillip pulled back. "Yes."

She must have looked dumbfounded, because he explained. "You were a student, and I was a teacher. Unethical on many levels, certainly, but the main reason I didn't act on the feeling then is that it would have been stereotypical, and that's something I refuse to be."

After that night, Sophia and Phillip saw each other almost daily over the next few months. She felt as if she was on an unending amusement park ride. He was spontaneous and often had wacky ideas, but they were always fun. One morning in March, he called her to suggest they go to Joshua Tree that night to watch a certain constellation of the planets.

"It's a new moon in Pisces, and we'll be able to see the big dipper," he said.

They set out at eight after Sophia finished with her last client of the day. Rather than come up like he usually did, Phillip honked his horn.

She ran out of her apartment and slid into his car, her heart filling with joy at the sight of him like it always did.

"I brought us some coffee and croissants," he said, handing her a bag as he put the car in gear.

Two hours later, they arrived at Joshua tree, the moon bright in the sky, the giant, up-reaching yuccas casting formidable shadows in the silvery light. Phillip pulled off the highway and headed down a bumpy dirt road until they came to a clearing. He turned off the car and peered through the windshield up at the sky and smiled. "It's incredible how much clearer it is out here without all the smog."

They got out of the car, and Sophia glanced around at the quiet terrain. It was cold out here in the high desert at night. Though she wore a sweater and jeans, she shivered slightly. Phillip saw. "I've got a blanket in the trunk. Let me grab it."

When he returned with the blanket and shook it out onto the sandy ground, he sat and motioned for her. She slid into his arms, nestling up against his warm body, and looked up at the dazzling sky. "Now I see what all the fuss is about," she murmured. "The moon is so bright and beautiful out here, and the stars are the clearest I've ever seen."

He pulled her closer to him, and they sat there gazing up at the sky, quiet for a time. It was that way with them. Often nothing needed to be said. They simply reveled in each other's presence.

But tonight, Sophia sensed Phillip held something back. Finally, she asked, "Is everything okay?"

He sighed. "You know I'm in the National Guard."

"Of course, you go away once a month for training."

"I'm going away again, but this time it's not for training."

A heavy feeling settled in the pit of her stomach at his words. "What do you mean?"

"The war in Fallujah. President Bush has ordered National Guard troops to the region."

"But it's dangerous there."

"I know. This is something I agreed to when I signed up."

"But Phillip." Sophia felt tears spring to her eyes and tried to wipe them away with the back of her hand. This couldn't be happening.

"Shh," he said. "It'll be okay. I've been trained well."

"You don't know that it will be okay."

"I'm sorry Sophia," he said into her hair, his breath caressing the side of her neck. "The last thing I want to do is leave you."

"When do you go?" she asked, her voice a hoarse whisper.

"Next week, but let's not focus on that right now." He sought her lips with his then. Through tears, Sophia responded, something urging her to remember this night, this feeling. To remember him. Up until then they had only kissed; Phillip letting Sophia set the pace. In a bold move, she took his hands and guided them under her sweater, urging him to unclasp her bra. When his warm hands cupped her breasts, a need like she'd never felt overtook her. She reached for the zipper on his jeans.

Phillip's eyes stopped her. "Are you sure?" he asked, his voice low and throaty.

"I've never been surer of anything," said Sophia as she lay back on the blanket, the shower of stars above seeming as if they might rain down on them at any moment.

Chapter Six

S eptember 2, 2021, Orange, California

"Teddy, get up, you're going to be late."

Sophia's son's eyes opened, and he peered up at her. "What time is it?"

"It's 7:30."

He closed his eyes and groaned. "I don't have to be to school until 8:30, mom."

"I know, but this will give you some time to wake up. You don't want to walk into your first day as a senior looking like you're still asleep."

Teddy sighed and sat up on the side of the bed, then ruffled his hands through his unruly blond hair and yawned. "I'm sure I wouldn't be the only one. Can I have some coffee, at least?"

"I'll go make you some. Wear something decent, okay?"

Her son retorted as she headed out of the room, "As opposed to something indecent? Like what, my swim trunks?"

Sophia smiled at his comment, thinking about how he'd spent all summer swimming. Then she went to the kitchen where she reached into the cupboard for a bag of coffee. As she measured out the grounds, she thought about the fact that Teddy would soon be in college. She glanced over at the photo on the kitchen island of him when he was five, chubby cheeks and bright smile. The scent of coffee wafted throughout the two-bedroom condo when Teddy came in and climbed onto a stool at the kitchen island. Sophia eyed the blue polo and jeans with approval.

"I cooked you some eggs and hash browns," she said, pulling a plate out of the oven where she'd put it to keep warm. She had gotten up extra early, as if she were the one about to embark on her first day of school.

"Thanks," he said, nodding in approval, then began shoveling the food down. She watched as he ate, love for him washing through her.

"Slow down. I don't want to have to do the Heimlich maneuver this morning," she warned.

Her son glanced up and grinned mid-bite. "I thought you said you didn't want me to be late?"

"Funny, ha ha," she said, reaching for her coffee cup and taking a sip. "I'll be in the center with clients today, but I'll make sure to pick you up by three at the latest."

Teddy rolled his eyes. "I already told you I can get home by myself. I'm not five anymore. And once I'm eighteen in December, I'll be getting my car like you promised."

"Yes, you'll be getting your car, but let me hold onto your childhood just a little longer, okay?"

Teddy stopped eating and smiled. "So, this is a mom thing, then."

"Exactly. Now finish eating. I'm going to finish getting ready."

After dropping Teddy off at school, Sophia made her way to Kline Counseling, pulling into the parking space that read Dr. Strand. Once in the office, she was surprised to see that Cathy hadn't come in yet. She turned on the lights in the waiting room and started a pot of coffee for clients, then went into her office. Sitting behind her desk, which faced the doorway, she pulled out her cellphone and noticed she had a text from Cathy.

Hi Sophia, Chuck has been admitted to St. Joseph's. They think it might be a mild stroke. I have a new patient coming in. Her name is Dorothy Atwater. Can you take her? She was a referral.

Sophia tapped an answer: *Of course, please attend to Chuck. I'll take care of everything. Keep me posted.*

Then she set down her phone and sighed, jumping when it started ringing. She checked the screen to see a familiar number.

"Grandmother, is everything okay?"

"Does anything have to be wrong for me to call you?"

Sophia leaned back in her chair and relaxed her shoulders. "No, Cathy's husband was admitted to the ER, so I'm a little jumpy. It's so nice to hear your voice." She smiled, picturing her grandmother's kind face, her dark hair spun with gray pulled back by one of her colorful scarves.

"How are you doing, little love?"

"It was Teddy's first day of high school as a senior, so I'm a little melancholy, but it will pass."

"He's a young man now." There was silence on the end of the line for a moment, then her grandmother asked, "Did you read the book I sent?"

Sophia picked up a book sitting on the edge of her desk where she'd left it since opening the package. She read the title again: *Many Lives, Many Masters.*

"No, I haven't yet. It just came yesterday. So, the man who wrote the book is a psychotherapist, and it's about past lives. It sounds interesting. I'll read it soon and let you know."

"Good," said her grandmother. "The sooner, the better. You're going to need it." Then she changed the subject. "Since it's my turn to visit, I'm thinking of Christmas. Would that work?"

"That would be wonderful," said Sophia.

"I know it's only been a month since you and Teddy visited, but I'm ready to see my two favorite people again."

"We are, too." Sophia heard the front door chime. "I'm sorry, Grandmother, I need to go. A client has arrived."

Out in the waiting room, Sophia found a young woman standing in front of the door, her face pensive, her stance rigid. She wore a waitress uniform and held a purse up against her chest.

Sophia held out her hand. "I'm Dr. Sophia Strand. Dr. Harlan had a family emergency and couldn't be here. You must be Dorothy. I'll be seeing you today."

The woman continued to clutch her purse, eyeing Sophia. "You're a doctor?"

"I have my doctorate in psychology. I've been working with Dr. Harlan for nearly two decades. I'm able to help you with your problem."

Dorothy shook her head. "I don't know if anyone can help me with my problem, but okay, what do I do?"

Sophia smiled and pointed to the hallway. "Let's go to my office. You can fill out some intake paperwork. Then we'll discuss how I might help you."

In her office, Sophia handed the young woman a clipboard. "Just fill out the front of the first page giving me your contact information and that sort of thing. No need to enter why you're here. We can talk about that in a minute."

When Dorothy finished, Sophia scanned the form. "So, you live in Santa Ana currently, and you're twenty-four. You have a woodworking certificate from Santa Ana College. Have you always wanted to be a carpenter?"

Dorothy's eyes brightened. "Yes, since I was a kid. My dad taught me. He was a professional carpenter. He made furniture. I prefer to do smaller pieces, like signs, and I recently made a jewelry box for a client that I also carved." She glanced down at her uniform. "I'm not making as much as I need, so I also waitress on the side."

"The jewelry box sounds beautiful. You said your father was a carpenter. Did he pass?"

The woman cleared her throat. "Yes, a couple of years ago."

Sophia pointed to the couch on the other side of the room next to the blue wall. "Let's talk over there if you don't mind. Rather than having the desk between us."

After Dorothy got settled on the couch and Sophia in an armchair across from her, she waited for the young woman to speak. After a few moments of silence, Sophia said, "It's difficult when a loved one passes. It takes time to mourn the loss. Tell me about your father."

Dorothy looked down at her lap where her hands were clasped

tightly. Then she met Sophia's eyes and blurted, "Have you ever had your palms read?"

Sophia shifted in her seat, unsure where this was going. "No, I don't think I have."

"I saw a palm reader a few months ago. She told me some things that..." Dorothy trailed off.

"Some things about your father?"

"No." Dorothy took a deep breath, then spoke. "Have you ever had *déjà vu*?"

"I think everyone has at some point in time had that feeling, yes."

"Well, there's this guy I met two weeks ago. The palm reader said I'd be meeting him, and that I'd have major feelings of *déjà vu*. I just figured it was her gimmick, and I forgot all about it, until I met someone."

Sophia let a good thirty seconds pass, then spoke. "It can feel unsettling when that happens."

"It was more than unsettling," said Dorothy. "It's hard to explain, but I feel like we know each other, even though we only talked for an hour at this party I went to. Since then, I'm having a hard time sleeping and eating and thinking even."

Sophia glanced at Dorothy's records. No indication of medication for any mental health disorders.

"I'm not crazy, Dr. Strand. Before this happened, I was fine. I've never even been to a psychiatrist or counselor or whatever it is you are. I know this sounds insane, but something about meeting him triggered something in me. I came here because I didn't know where else to turn. I'm sure what I'm saying makes no sense to you. I'm sorry I bothered you." Dorothy picked up her purse and stood.

The book on the edge of her desk in her peripheral vision, Sophia raised a hand and urged, "Please, have a seat. I'll admit that what you're saying does sound strange, but on the other hand, it makes perfect sense."

Chapter Seven

Dorothy's eyes widened. "You mean you believe me?"

Sophia measured her words carefully. "I believe you that something was triggered by meeting this man. What, I can't say, but I think it's worth giving counseling a chance to see if we can find out. You said it yourself, you don't know where else to turn. I'd like to see if I can help you."

Dorothy sat back down. "Okay."

"Let's start with you telling me what happened when you met."

"Sophia, my little love, what's the matter? I can barely hear you."

Sophia clutched the phone to her ear, trying to find her voice, hoarse from crying. "The man I told you about, Phillip, he left."

"Where did he go?"

"To war, Grandmother, to Fallujah. He's in America's national guard."

The silence on the other end of the phone made Sophia's tears stop. "Tell me he's coming back," she pleaded. "Please, Grandmother. I can't lose him."

"My little love," her grandmother said softly, the words Sophia longed to hear not passing her lips. "Take a deep breath."

She felt queasy in the stomach. "He's not coming back, is he?"

"We don't know that for sure," said her grandmother, her tone vague.

"But you know. You always know. Tell me."

"Have you heard from him?"

Sophia reached for a tissue and used it to dry her cheeks. "Yes, when he arrived, but nothing for a week now." Then she stood and walked to the window to look out, but the late afternoon sun hurt her eyes, and she turned away.

Her grandmother remained silent.

"The silly thing is," Sophia continued, "we've only been together for a few short months, but..." she trailed off.

"But you feel as if you've known one another forever," her grandmother finished her sentence. "You have, over many lifetimes. The sooner you can embrace and accept that, the better."

Sophia stamped her foot. "And then what? Will that bring Phillip home to me safe and sound? Why all this talk of old, forgotten lifetimes?" As soon as her outburst poured from her lips, Sophia felt badly. "I'm sorry, Grandmother, I know you mean well."

"It's okay, you are worried and scared, and confused," said her grandmother. "One thing I can tell you for certain. The lifetimes may be old, but they are never forgotten."

"So, you met Anre at a nightclub," said Sophia as she made notes about the man inhabiting Dorothy's every waking hour and dreams.

"Are you in the habit of meeting men in that way? I'm not meaning that as an admonishment. I'm just asking."

"Oh, my god, no, never!" said Dorothy. "This is what I'm talking about. I have been so unlike myself from the second I met him. I've made fun of women who troll bars for men."

Sophia stopped writing and met Dorothy's eyes. "What was it about Anre? What makes him different than other men?"

Dorothy threw up her hands and slapped them back down on her thighs. "I have been trying to figure that out. He's attractive, but I've dated men who are more handsome. To be honest, he isn't really my type. And he's French. Not that I have anything against that, but it's just so...random."

Sophia set the pen on her notepad and checked the clock. "It seems that there is something in the randomness that we need to untangle," she said, almost to herself. "Our time is just about up right now. How about we resume on Friday?"

Dorothy nodded. "I'd like that. Talking about Craig made me feel better somehow. Less crazy." She smiled and stood.

The comment stopped Sophia for a moment. "Dorothy, you just said talking about Craig. Do you know a Craig?"

A look of surprise crossed the girl's face. "I did? No, I don't know any Craigs. How odd." Then she shrugged. "But then this whole thing has been weird."

Sophia collected payment and walked with Dorothy to the waiting room. As she watched the girl leave through the front door, for a split-second, she saw her wearing a bright pink go-go outfit and thigh-high white boots. Then the image faded as quickly as it had come. Sophia checked her watch. She had an hour before the next client. She went back to her desk and sat down, picking up the book her grandmother had sent her and pulling out the note tucked inside. Sophia read the message, written in her grandmother's elegant handwriting. *It will follow you, little love. You know this. It always catches up. My advice? Run to it. Only then will you have peace. This is important for you and those you will soon be helping.* Sophia sat back and began reading about the psychotherapist who had helped many of his patients with past life regression therapy.

. . .

Sophia pulled up at the school at three that afternoon. She searched the sidewalk for Teddy, breathing a sigh of relief when she spotted him talking to another student. She had thought when he got older, she would stop feeling panicked when she didn't immediately find him at pickup, but it still happened. When he saw her, he waved and smiled, then loped toward her, his backpack thumping against his side. He surprised her by pulling open the passenger side door and climbing in next to her.

"I'm not chauffeuring you today. Isn't that uncool?"

Teddy shrugged. "That was middle school, mom, I'm in high school now."

"Don't remind me. How was your first day?" Sophia asked as she pulled away from the curb and got behind a line of cars inching their way out of the school parking lot.

"It was good. A lot less rules and regulations. I guess they figure we don't need to be monitored constantly now that we're almost out of there."

"I'd say that's a good thing. How about making pizza tonight? I have to stop by the grocery store. We could get some of those energy drinks you like, too."

Teddy reached over and turned on the car's AC. "Sounds good to me, as long as we get some pineapple."

"In that case, it's personal pizzas," said Sophia. "No pineapple is getting near my pepperoni."

When they pulled into Albertsons parking lot and got out of the car and began walking toward the store, Sophia was struck once again at how much Teddy had grown. He had to have shot up several inches over the summer. Just as they neared the grocery store doors, she caught a glimpse of her son reflected in the glass and nearly gasped at how much he looked like his father.

"Sophia, it's late there. Any word?"

"No, Grandmother, please tell me what you see. I must know. I feel as if I'm losing my mind."

"It's best you wait and find out through normal channels."

"I just want him to return. To come home to me. We had so little time together. I don't think I can go on without him." Sophia felt so flattened, so hopeless, so desperate for any word from Phillip.

"You will and you can go on, Sophia. You are strong." Her grandmother's tone was uncharacteristically strident. "And you will need that strength in the coming days and months."

"What does that mean?"

"Just lie down and rest, little love," her grandmother said more softly. "I'll send you some healing energy."

Chapter Eight

"We're going to try something known as regression therapy today," said Sophia at Dorothy's next session.

"What's that?"

Sophia glanced at the book on her desk, which she'd now read in its entirety. She debated how much to tell her.

"We're going to see what you have stored in your subconscious about you and Anre."

The young woman blinked. "But I told you, we've only just met."

She eyed Dorothy, who appeared unrested and disheveled. "Our subconscious can hide certain information from us. It could be that Anre is triggering something in you that originated in childhood. Regressing back in time could show us what that was so you can work your way through this."

The young woman's shoulders relaxed. "Well, that sounds great. Because the guy is avoiding me now, and I just want him out of my head."

"Why don't you lie down?" Sophia suggested. "I think this method will work better if you're relaxed."

Just then a phone buzzed, and Dorothy apologized. "I'm sorry. I thought for sure I'd turned my cell off." She dug around in her purse and pulled it out, then checked the screen. "OMG. It's him. What do I do?"

Sophia considered the question, reminding herself that becoming enmeshed in patient's lives was not a good idea.

Dorothy read the text out loud. "*Thinking of you. How are you?*" She slapped the phone down on the couch. "What is wrong with this guy? He ignores my texts for two days, and now this?"

"Why don't you shut off the phone, and let's focus on you. You can always text him later, if you choose to."

Dorothy nodded. "You're so right." She powered off her phone and dropped it in her purse. "Like I said, I literally have not been myself since all of this started." She made herself comfortable on the sofa. "I'm ready."

Sophia set the app on her phone to play the sound of light rain and dimmed the overhead light, then began.

"Take several deep breaths. As you do so, let the air flow out your body, fingers and toes. Picture the air as gray or even black as it leaves your body, taking all tension and anxiety from you. Breathing, breathing, breathing. Your only task at this point in time is to breathe. Now we will begin muscle relaxation starting at the shoulders, feel them slumping down as you sink into the couch. Breathing, breathing. Now we focus on easing tension in your chest."

Ten minutes later, Dorothy appeared to be in a deep, meditative state. "Now we're going to take a journey back in time to the first place that your subconscious wishes to show us," said Sophia softly. "We're going to walk through a series of doorways. You'll see one doorway in particular in the distance that is purple. That is the doorway you will pass through where you will see what you came here today to see. Slowly, slowly, you are nearing the doorway. When you arrive, reach out and turn the handle and open the door and step through. Tell me what you see when you enter."

At first, Sophia thought she may have fallen asleep, but then Dorothy spoke, her voice more high-pitched and girlish than before. "I walked through the door."

Sophia leaned forward to watch as Dorothy's eyes moved rapidly below the lids. "What do you see, Dorothy?" she said quietly.

"My name is not Dorothy," she said sharply, startling Sophia. "It is Clarisse."

Sophia's heart sped up. "Okay, Clarisse, what do you see around you?"

She cupped her hands on her ears. "It's loud in here, and the strobe lights always make me feel dizzy."

Sophia quickly scribbled a few notes on her pad. "Where are you?"

"I'm at the club," she said, her tone annoyed. "And I'm on in twenty."

"On where?"

"I'm a go-go dancer," she said, as if Sophia should know. "I've got to find the manager. He owes me money. I refuse to keep working here without getting paid."

Sophia watched as Dorothy scowled. She almost didn't look like herself.

"What's happening now, Clarisse?" Sophia asked after some time passed.

"Have you seen Marvin?"

Sophia waited, fascinated. The girl appeared to be having a conversation with someone.

"I get paid now, or I'm not going on."

After a few beats, Sophia asked, "Did you get paid?"

"I did, finally. It's ten bucks short, but, okay, fine."

"Are you going on?" asked Sophia.

"I have to put on my makeup, but the lighting is terrible in this shit hole."

Sophia waited, watching as Dorothy's demeanor gradually changed, and she became more relaxed. Finally, she asked her, "Are you performing now?"

Dorothy smiled. "Yes."

The lights refracted around the room as Clarisse wiggled her hips and pumped her arms. She was on a platform overlooking a crowd of mostly men. Their claps and whistles fueled her. So intent was she on dancing that it was some time before she spotted the man watching her from the sidelines. She looked into his eyes and couldn't peel them away as she finished her set. When she was done and it was time to climb down from the stage, he appeared suddenly, his hand extended.

"Need some help?" he asked, his green eyes laughing.

Clarisse hesitated to take his hand. What was his game?

"I'm okay," she said, her heart thundering in her chest—and it was from more than the dancing.

"I won't bite." He smiled, his teeth straight and white, his brown hair in a ponytail. "Your dancing was groovy."

"Clarisse, Samantha's up, you need to get down!" called out Marvin.

She held out her hand to the mystery man, who reached up and grabbed her by the waist, pulling her to the floor within inches of him. Unnerved as the heat of their bodies met, Clarisse stepped back. "Thank you. I need to get to the dressing room."

"Wait, before you go," he said. "What's your name?"

"It's Clarisse," she said over her shoulder.

"I'm Craig," he called after her. "I'm sure I'll be seeing you around."

When Dorothy uttered the name Craig, she appeared distressed. "Let's focus on your breathing now," said Sophia. "It's time to come back to the here and now. Walk back out the doorway and head down the path away from the purple door. Listen to the sound of my voice as it guides you. I'm going to count backward from ten. When I reach one, you will be back here in 2017. Ten, nine, eight, seven, six, five, four, three, two, one. Now open your eyes. You are back in Orange."

Dorothy's eyes fluttered open, and she turned her head toward Sophia. "What just happened?"

"Tell me what you remember."

"I was in some sort of a club. There were a lot of flashing lights, and the music was loud." She sat up slowly and touched her hands to her jeans. "I was wearing thigh-high white boots, and a pink dress." Her face registered confusion as she looked into Sophia's eyes. "I was dancing, but it was a place I don't recognize." She ran her hands through her hair. "Is this normal when you put someone into a meditative state?"

Sophia nodded. "Yes, these are memories buried in your psyche. Do you remember what happened right before you came back?"

Dorothy thought for a moment, then gasped. "Oh, my god. There was a man watching me dance." Her eyes widened. "He called himself Craig, but it was Anre."

Chapter Nine

Sophia let what Dorothy said sink in for a moment before speaking. "I told you that we were regressing you to uncover items in your psyche. The truth is a little more complicated. We were regressing you to..." Sophia paused, thinking how crazy this all sounded, then resumed, "To take you to a past life."

"A what?"

Sophia placed the pad on the table next to her. "It looks like you and Anre have known each other in prior lifetimes."

Dorothy seemed contemplative for a moment, and then replied, "I can't believe I'm going to say this, but that's the first thing anyone has said about this situation that makes sense."

Sophia, who had been braced for blowback, sat up straighter, surprised. "It does?"

"Yes. Ever since I met Anre, I felt like I knew him. But it sounded too crazy to say out loud, so I didn't. I kept thinking back in my life, wondering if we'd ever met at some point, and the answer was always no. The night we met, he also said something."

"What did he say?"

"He said, *déjà vu*. And he looked at me oddly. I remember thinking it was a weird statement. But the moment passed, and we moved on to something else. We talked for hours that first night, like we'd known each other forever. And then things got weird."

"Weird how?"

"As I mentioned, I started dreaming about him. And I didn't mention to you that some of the dreams were quite disturbing. And then he started ghosting me."

Sophia was about to respond when the timer she set at the beginning of their session sounded. "I'm afraid we've run out of time. And I have someone right after you. Hold those thoughts until next time."

Sophia awoke after a restless night to bleak morning sunshine stealing in from under the curtain by her bed. She listened to her own breathing, slow and measured. That's what she'd had to do recently, in order not to implode. Focus on taking each moment by moment. The worry brought on by waiting for word about Phillip had drained her. She slept, but she woke up as tired, or even more tired, than when she went to bed. In the bathroom, she splashed cold water on her face, then checked out her reflection, dark smudges under her eyes. She went to her closet and pulled it open, surveying the bare contents. She hadn't had the energy to do laundry in a while. Pulling out the only remaining outfit appropriate for the counseling office, she put on the black skirt and green blouse and went to the kitchen. The idea of food turned her stomach, so she made herself a cup of tea, then pulled open the front door and picked up the newspaper. She slid off the string and unfolded it, her heart lurching at the headline. *More Americans wounded in Iraq.*

It was two weeks before Dorothy and Sophia had another session. The woman's mother had been in the hospital.

"How are you doing today?" asked Sophia as she gestured for her to take the couch.

Dorothy sat down and put her head in her hands. "I've had better days and weeks."

"How is your mother?" Sophia reached for her notepad and sat facing her.

Dorothy sighed. "She's going to be okay, thank goodness. But I'm a little sleep deprived from spending a bunch of nights in the hospital with her."

"That is tough," said Sophia. "I'm very glad to hear she's going to be okay, though."

Dorothy appeared thoughtful. "Is it possible that my mother and I also have a past life together? I'm asking because we're so close and always have been."

"From what I've read on the topic, yes, it's quite possible," said Sophia. "In fact, we tend to reincarnate in what they call soul groups, and as such we reincarnate with the same souls again and again."

Dorothy laughed for the first time since they had met. "I can't imagine wanting to reincarnate with my sister! She's been such a pain since mom got sick."

Sophia smiled. "Are you ready to try another regression?"

Dorothy nodded her head vigorously.

"Are you going to invite me in?"

Clarisse stood in front of her apartment door, key in hand. She and Craig had gone out for coffee after her set at the club. She was wired, but not sure she wanted to let him in just yet. She liked him, but after her last experience with Bernard, she was more than gun-shy.

"I've got an early day tomorrow," she said. "Maybe next time?"

Craig looked disappointed but smiled and backed up. "Of course. Have a good night." He waited while Clarisse went into her apartment. As soon as she shut the door, she reconsidered. What would be the harm in inviting him in for a while? She pulled open the door, ready to call after him, but saw no one on the quiet sidewalk at midnight. She started to close the door when a boot suddenly appeared in the doorway.

"You were out late," growled Bernard. He smelled of beer and sweat.

"It's none of your business what I'm doing. We're not together anymore," said Clarisse, kicking at his boot as she tried to shut the door.

"Is he your new boyfriend?"

Clarisse was becoming increasingly uncomfortable with the look in Bernard's eyes. She'd seen it before. That last night. "Chelsea will be home soon," she told him, trying to keep her tone steady. "You need to leave, Bernard."

He leered at her and with one swift push sent her flying into the apartment. She fell onto her back and skidded across the floor.

Bernard slammed the door and came to tower over her as she scrambled to her feet. "You look like a slut in that outfit." He grabbed her, pulling her up against him, his mouth claiming hers. When she shuddered at his touch and pushed against his chest with her palms, he pulled his head back and glowered at her, his eyes brittle, his large hands tightening their grip on her arms. "You're too good for me now?"

When Dorothy screamed, Sophia said sharply, "It's time to come back now. I'm going to count backwards from ten, and you're going to be back here in Orange."

To Sophia's relief, Dorothy soon opened her eyes and seemed to recognize her.

"That was the past. You're safe," said Sophia, wondering now if regressing was such a good idea. "Are you okay, Dorothy?"

"When I was Clarisse, Bernard raped me," she said.

Chapter Ten

Dorothy looked like she'd just run a marathon. Sophia got her a glass of water and waited while she took several sips. She set the glass in her lap and took a deep breath. "I've always wondered why I've been so afraid to be with a man. I'm twenty-four and still a virgin." She blushed. "Boyfriends have wanted to be intimate, but I've been afraid for some reason. Now I know why."

"This is a lot to process," said Sophia. "Take your time."

"But it doesn't explain one thing. Why the push and pull between me and Anre?" She glanced at the clock on the wall. "We have some more time. Can you put me back under so I can see what happened?"

Sophia was unsure, given how traumatic the experience had just been. "I don't know if that is such a good idea, Dorothy."

"I'm okay, really. In a strange way, I feel lighter. Like you said, that was before. It's not my life now."

Sophia considered for a moment, noting that Dorothy did appear more relaxed. Perhaps this was actually helping. "Okay, but if you start to get upset, I'm pulling you out right away."

Clarisse must have passed out, because she awoke suddenly in the middle of her entryway floor alone. She felt terrible pain in her abdomen and tried to sit up but couldn't. Just then the front door opened, and she heard Chelsea's voice. "Oh, my god, Clarisse. What happened? Mitch, call 911!"

Her friend's concerned face hovered above Clarisse as she tried to talk. "Shh," said Chelsea. "The paramedics will be here soon."

"It was Ber..." Clarisse struggled to tell her friend.

"Bernard?" asked Chelsea.

"Yes," said Clarisse, closing her eyes as her roommate's voice faded away. When the sirens stopped in front of the apartment complex, Clarisse felt herself slip from her body. She heard disembodied voices and watched from above as the paramedics tried to revive her. Clarisse wanted to reach out and soothe Chelsea, who kept wailing her name, but it was time to head to the beautiful light beckoning her.

When Sophia realized that Dorothy was experiencing her own death as Clarisse, she panicked and pulled her back immediately. As she waited for the girl to return to the present, she held her breath and prayed. "Dorothy, it's time to come back to the now," Sophia repeated. "You're safe. That lifetime is over."

Dorothy opened her eyes and smiled, a faraway expression in her eyes. "How beautiful," she murmured.

Sophia was shocked. "What was beautiful?"

Dorothy appeared more serene and calm than Sophia had seen her until now. "My death. I was floating above my body. It felt so..." she trailed away, appearing at a loss for words. Then she looked at Sophia, her eyes glistening with unshed tears. "Thank you, Dr. Strand. I feel much better. This answered so many questions for me. Even with Anre."

"How's that?" asked Sophia.

Dorothy sat up. "Think about it. If he lost me back then in such a horrible way, that explains why he is acting so strange now. His conscious mind doesn't know what it is, but at a soul level, he knows what happened."

Sophia blinked at the depth of Dorothy's words, realizing how they echoed her grandmother's comments over the years. "What are you going to do with this information?" she asked Dorothy.

"I'm going to call Anre and try to talk to him. I ignored the text I read you that he sent a couple of weeks ago, and then I got involved in what was happening with my mother. I'm hoping he'll hear me out."

"Will you tell him what you know about this?" asked Sophia.

"I'm going to try. He did mention *de ja vu*, so this isn't too far from that." The more she spoke, the more peaceful Dorothy became. "And now I know that some of the odd fears that have held me back aren't even from this life." Her face brightened. "This is absolutely amazing, Dr. Strand. You have no idea how life changing what you're doing is."

Later that day when it was early morning in Greece, Sophia called her grandmother.

"Little love, is all well, you are calling me early."

Sophia knew that her grandmother had some pain these days from arthritis. She pictured her sitting in the sun on her balcony, which she said warmed her muscles and bones.

"All is well, grandmother. Thank you for the book. I used the knowledge to help a patient. I see now what you've been telling me all these years. I can't believe I didn't listen before."

"All in the exact right time," said her grandmother. "Speaking of, tell me, how is my handsome grandson?"

Sophia smiled. "He is enjoying being a senior. I can't believe he turns eighteen in December. Time has gone so fast, and yet..." she hesitated.

"So slow," her grandmother finished her sentence. "We are always with those we love," she said. "I think you see that more clearly now. The work you will do with your clients, it is of vital importance."

When she hung up the phone with her grandmother, Sophia was going to make final notes on Dorothy's sessions in her office but decided to take advantage of the late afternoon sunshine at the nearby park. She sat down on her favorite bench under a giant liquidambar tree and took out her pen when two mourning doves flew overhead, side-by-side, their wings flapping in unison. Their fluidity struck her—and then the memory flooded in.

It was Phillip's last day before deployment, and they had decided to take a picnic to the park. Sophia prepared the feast—piling subs high with cold cuts and tomatoes and making her grandmother's brand of Greek-style Cole slaw with feta and carrot. The early afternoon was crisp and cool, so she had worn her pink cardigan over Phillip's favorite dress, a white cotton print covered in roses. As they set up their picnic, she got on her hands and knees to straighten the edges of the blanket, all the while holding back tears. She had wanted to enjoy this day but was having a hard time balancing that desire with the heavy feeling of dread she felt deep in her stomach. As she pressed the corners of the blanket into the moist earth, Phillip spoke to her softly. "That's good enough, Sophia."

She stood, wiping dirt off her hands and faced him, the tears she'd been holding back spilling now. He grabbed a napkin from the pile she'd put on the blanket and handed it to her. "We'll always be together, even when I'm not here, my love," he said. "I've known that since the day we met."

Sophia gulped back another torrent of tears. "I'm sorry. I didn't want to do this today. It's just that..." She looked away, watching two children running after a ball in the distance, then pulled her eyes back to his. "I don't have a good feeling about this, Phillip."

He was about to respond when a slight whoosh filled the air around them and the sky darkened momentarily. They both looked up to see two mourning doves flying away in tandem.

Chapter Eleven

When Sophia finalized her notes on Dorothy's sessions, she gazed out over the trees in the distance, thinking about all the synchronicities that came up during their sessions. While some of what had been brought forth by Dorothy could have been coincidental, she didn't see how the young woman could have relayed so many details about what it was like to be a go-go dancer in the 1960s.

She spent another fifteen minutes checking emails on her phone, then gathered her things to head home to Teddy when her cellphone rang. "This is Dr. Strand."

"Hi, my name is Benjamin," said a tentative voice. "I got your name from Dorothy Atwater."

"Hi, Benjamin, how can I help you?"

He cleared his throat. "Dorothy told me about how you helped her with her past life. I'd like to make an appointment. Could I possibly see you tomorrow morning?"

When the call came, Sophia was prepared. Something had woken her at midnight. She had bolted up to see a white, fuzzy figure at the foot of her bed. For a moment, it formed into a person, then faded away.

She got out of bed then and went to sit in a chair by the window, eventually watching the sunrise. As the morning cast its watery light into her living room, Sophia's phone rang. Putting the receiver to her ear, she waited.

"Sophia?" It was Cathy.

"Yes."

"I'm sorry, but Phillip is..." Her voice became strangled, "gone."

Sophia had cried throughout the night, and her eyes were now dry. "When?"

"Several hours ago. About midnight our time. An IED hit the jeep he was in." Sophia heard sobbing on the other end of the line. "I'm sorry, I need to go. I just thought you should know."

Sophia's next call was to her grandmother, who picked up the phone, the sound of voices in the background.

"Sophia, excuse the chatter, I'm having a dinner party."

"He's gone, Grandmother, but I'm sure you knew that was going to happen."

Her grandmother was quiet on the other end of the line, then finally spoke. "You'll be okay, little love. I promise you."

"If I'm going to be okay, why do I feel like my heart has been ripped from my chest and run over?" Anger at Phillip welled in Sophia for coming into her life and leaving so suddenly.

"There is much more to your life, but first you must grieve," said her grandmother. "I will come to you. I can be on a flight tomorrow morning."

Sophia was about to protest, but the truth was, she desperately wanted to see her grandmother.

· · ·

When her grandmother rapped on her door the following evening, Sophia pulled it open. The older woman set down her suitcase in the entryway and took her granddaughter in her arms. Sophia began weeping, her cries filling the hallway.

"Let's get inside," said her grandmother, gently shutting the door and leading Sophia to the sofa. "You look like you haven't slept in days, and that's not good for you. You must keep up your strength. I'm going to make you some soup. For now, just lie down and rest."

"I don't have any food in the house," said Sophia, another wave of tears beginning to surface.

"I will go to the store and buy some things. For now, just close your eyes and get some sleep."

Sophia looked up at her grandmother, whose expression appeared grave. "Why does it matter if I ever sleep again? Phillip is gone. I'd rather leave and join him. The worst part is, I always knew. From the moment he told me he was leaving, I knew he wouldn't return."

Her grandmother knelt and brushed her hair from her forehead and kissed her. "It's not your time. You have many important things left to do in this lifetime. Close your eyes now."

Sophia awoke later that night to the smell of chicken soup. She sat up to see her grandmother in the apartment's small kitchen.

"Your soup is ready," she said, without looking up. "Let me bring you some."

Her grandmother bustled over with a giant earthenware bowl of homemade soup, setting it down on the coffee table along with a sleeve of saltines. As the aroma wafted toward her, Sophia suddenly felt famished. Her grandmother watched with approval as she crushed a handful of crackers on top of the soup and tentatively took a spoonful of the delicious, warm liquid. Sophia ate the entire bowl, then handed it to her grandmother.

"Would you like more?"

Sophia shook her head. "No, that was the perfect amount. Thank you." It was then that she noticed for the first time a paper bag on the coffee table. "What's that?"

"Just something you need. I picked it up when I was out." She took the bowl to the kitchen sink and turned on the tap.

Sophia reached for the bag and opened it, gasping at the contents. She pulled out the pregnancy test and looked at her grandmother, who met her eyes. After some moments passed, the only sound in the room a clock ticking on the wall, Sophia rose from the couch, box in hand, and went to the bathroom. When she came out a few minutes later, the wand in her hand, her grandmother smiled. "I think he will be a December baby."

Sophia eyed the plus on the wand. "He?"

Her grandmother came to face Sophia, putting her hands on her granddaughter's shoulders. "That is what I am seeing. You will soon have a healthy son to raise, little love."

For the first time in days, Sophia smiled, her heart filling with hope. "Phillip's son. Our son," she said.

After Teddy went to bed that night and the condo was quiet, the only sound an occasional car swooshing by on the street outside, Sophia pulled a photo album out of the credenza in the living room. She sat on the couch and opened it, the plastic cover crackling as she did so. There in faded color were Sophia and Phillip arm in arm in front of the university. She traced his face with her finger and murmured, "Teddy is so much like you. How I wish you could have met him."

Hours later after dozing off on the couch, Sophia awoke. She was about to go into her bedroom when a silhouette appeared beside the couch. Her eyes sticky with sleep, she tried to focus. The figure raised a hand and quietly said, "I am with you and Teddy always, my love. I had to go so that you could do what you are meant to do, but I am never far." Sophia shook herself awake and sat up, but the figure had vanished.

The next morning as she waited in line to get out of the parking lot after dropping off Teddy, her phone pinged. She pulled it out of her purse and checked the screen. It was from Dorothy. She smiled as she read the text. *Dr. Strand, you won't believe it but I've worked everything out with Anre! We talked for hours last night, and it turns out that he believes in past lives, and now he understands what happened with us. Thank you so much!*

Ten minutes later, Sophia approached the counseling office to find a man standing in front of the door. He was about thirty-five and had close-cropped hair and the upright stance of someone in the military. "Are you Benjamin?" she asked as she pulled out her office keys.

"Yes, are you Dr. Strand?"

"I am," she said as she unlocked the front door. "I hope you haven't been waiting too long and that I'm not late for our appointment."

"I'm early," he said when she beckoned him inside and flipped on the lights in the waiting room.

"Okay, well, let me get the lights turned on in my office, and then we can get started. Would you like some coffee? I can make some."

"I've already had too much this morning, ma'am, but thank you."

"Very well. Take a seat, and I'll be out for you shortly."

When she returned five minutes later, she found Benjamin sitting on the edge of a chair, looking as if he might bolt at any moment.

"You can come back to my office now," she said, prompting him to quickly stand and follow her.

In her office, she pointed to the chair across from her desk. "Make yourself comfortable. So, how do you know Dorothy?"

"We live in the same apartment complex." He stopped and sat up straighter. "Frankly, ma'am, what I'm going to tell you is going to sound...the only word for it is crazy. And the problem is, I can't do crazy. I've got high-security clearance." He shifted in his seat uncomfortably.

Sophia took a deep breath. "By that I think you mean military clearance. As you know, what we say here is protected by privilege, but given your circumstances, I understand your hesitancy. That being said, I'm guessing Benjamin isn't your real name?"

He looked at the floor, his face reddening, then back into her eyes. "No, ma'am. Is that going to be a problem?"

"If you're paying with cash, it won't be."

"I was planning to do just that."

"Okay, then. How can I help you?"

"Dorothy said that you did some kind of recall therapy on her?"

"It's known as past life regression therapy," said Sophia. "Seeing prior lifetimes can help people understand and heal issues in this lifetime."

He let out a long breath. "I think that's what I need."

"Tell me the situation," said Sophia, pen poised over her notepad.

"There's a woman I met several months ago. She's a bit older than me. We, I guess you could say, are in a relationship, but it's been a rollercoaster. To tell you the truth, I really should end it. It's not been good for my career. But there's something about her. About the way we are together." He tapped his foot on the floor several times, then resumed. "Full disclosure, we drink too much when we're together. And on several occasions, I've seen things."

When Benjamin didn't continue, Sophia prompted him. "What kind of things?"

"I think they're visions. They're of her and me, but not now. It's us in another lifetime."

"What sort of a lifetime?"

Benjamin shook his head and turned toward the door, as if checking to see if someone was eavesdropping. Then he turned back to Sophia. "Like I said, this is going to sound crazy. I'm seeing us at the circus, but we're not watching, we're in it. She is a trapeze artist, and I'm the lion tamer, and then there's this other man, and I'm pretty sure he is her husband."

"Is she married in this lifetime?"

"No, but she was. And it was a nasty breakup. She claims he's been stalking her. Like I said, I should really just extricate myself from this mess, but something is holding me back. I'm hoping you can help with that."

"I can certainly try."

Find out what happens next for Sophia and Benjamin in **book 2, *Suspended: Enforcement.***

A Note For You

Dear Reading Gem,

Thanks for spending time with me and Sophia!

Fates collide with destinies in The Past Life Prism Series. Starring Sophia Strand, a past life regression therapist, the series chronicles the torrid tales of significant relationships spanning centuries. Watch romance kindled, sparks fly, and intrigue unveiled as couples reunite in present day.

If you like the series, please leave a review or just stars on any book review platform. Your opinion matters and is incredibly powerful.

Thanks again and talk soon!

Stay Enlightened

Thanks for reading! Let's stay in touch. I post insider information, and sneak peeks of upcoming books on my website at https://www.juliebaw dendavis.com/fiction. You can also email me at Julie@JulieBawden Davis.com, find me on Facebook, and follow me on Amazon.

Even better, join my weekly VIP Reading Gems newsletter here. When signing up, you get a free copy of *Discovered Beginnings*, the prequel novella to my Discovered Truth Series. There are also lots of giveaways and contests!

Escape to Unforgettable Romance and Intrigue...

Books by Julie Bawden-Davis

The Past Life Prism Series
(Romantic Time Travel Suspense)
Suspended: The Beginning
Suspended Enforcement
Suspended Entrapment
Suspended Exodus
Suspended Entanglement

The Discovered Truth Series
(Romantic Suspense)
Discovered Beginnings:
(FREE at https://www.juliebawdendavis.com/fiction)
Discovered Secrets
Discovered Memories
Discovered Indiscretions
Discovered Liaisons
Discovered Betrayal
Discovered Denial
Discovered Distractions
Discovered Deception
Discovered Lies

Discovered Vengeance
Discovered Redemption
Discovered Obsession
Discovered Transgressions
Discovered Suspicion
Discovered Escape
Discovered Promises
Discovered Cover-Up
Discovered Intentions

www.ingramcontent.com/pod-product-compliance
Lightning Source LLC
Chambersburg PA
CBHW020335130626
46549CB00003B/1190